The Story Dance

Barbara Satterfield

illustrated by Fran Gregory

Fairview Press
Minneapolis

Library of Congress Cataloging-in-Publication Data

Satterfield, Barbara.
  The story dance / Barbara Satterfield ; illustrated by Fran Gregory.
       p.   cm.
  Summary: A young girl enjoys looking at the family treasures with her grandmother and hearing about the adventures of a great-aunt she has never known, especially about when Aunt Emmadelle learned to dance the flamenco in Spain.
  ISBN 1-57749-022-3
  [1. Grandmothers—Fiction. 2. Great-aunts—Fiction. 3. Heirlooms—Fiction.] I. Gregory, Fran, ill. II. Title
  PZ7.S24923St   1997   96-38688
  [E]—dc20   CIP
                                                                                      AC

Edited and designed by Robyn Hansen
Cover design by Circus Design

First Printing: April 1997
Printed in the United States of America

01 00 99 98 97   7 6 5 4 3 2 1

Published by Fairview Press, 2450 Riverside Avenue South, Minneapolis, MN 55454.

For a current catalog of Fairview Press titles, please call this Toll-Free number: 1-800-544-8207.

Publisher's Note: Fairview Press publishes books and other materials related to the subjects of family and social issues. Its publications, including *The Story Dance,* do not necessarily reflect the philosophy of Fairview Hospital and Healthcare Services or their treatment programs.

The paper used in this publication meets the minimum requirements of American National Standard for Information Sciences—Permanence of Paper for Printed Library Materials, ANSI Z329.48-1984.

In memory of my grandmother,
Marion Jane McAdams Laird

When I go to visit my grandmother, Nana, I like to look at the family treasures. She keeps them locked up in a tall, glass-front cabinet. They are special and fragile and older than she is. She shows them to me whenever I ask it. She tells me their stories as long as I'll listen. But I have been strictly forbidden to touch them, play with them, or hold them—those are the rules. But this time will be different.

"Nana," I say, "let's look at the treasures."

"My, my . . . " she says with a smile.

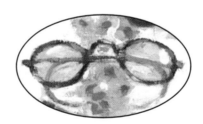

She opens the doors with a skeleton key and
lets me look over the shelves. I see her grandmother's glasses, a tiny wooden ring, the gold
stripes from grandfather's war uniform. A neck-
lace of buttons, an old valentine, a locket with
pictures and snips of curled hair. A baby cup,
books, and a pearl-handled knife. A loving cup
won at the county horse race. And my favorite
treasure for all-time forever—my great-aunty
Emmadelle's pink beaded shawl, lying next to a
photograph of strangely dressed people who posed
for a camera so long ago.

"This one," I say.

"Oh, you know that story," Nana says gently. "You know it by heart."

"But I've never heard it while holding the shawl," I say. "May I have a turn?"

"It isn't for handling," she says. "It might rip."

"But this year I'm eight. I know to be careful."

"My, my . . . I guess we can try."

Together we lift the shawl from the shelf. The beads clickety-click as it unfolds. A sheet of silk sewn up in flowers and peacocks, it slips through our fingers and falls on the floor.

Nana got it from Emmadelle, who crossed the wide ocean to study folk dances in faraway places. She met with the dancers and watched them, then wrote down their movements and noted the music.

"Go on," I say.

"Oh, you know what's next," Nana says laughing. "You know it by heart."

"But I've never heard it while wearing the shawl as the story is told," I say very slowly.

"It isn't for dress-up," she says. "It's too special."

"I will only wear it today, if you'll let me."

"Just once," Nana says. "Then we'll make another, one you can wear whenever you want to. My, my . . . how will it tie?"

Emmadelle met with some Gypsies in Spain to learn the folk dance they called the flamenco. She said the dancers made up their own steps, depending on how they felt at the time. Along with guitar music and castanets, they moved like a summer storm coming and going—hot sunlight and wind, slow thunder, quick lightning.

"And then," I say, "they danced."

"Exactly," says Nana. "You know it by heart."

"But I've never heard it while dancing each part, in the shawl, like a Gypsy," I say.

"It isn't for play," she says. "It's too delicate."

"I'll dance so gently," I promise in a whisper.

"Please do," Nana says. "But before you begin, we'll find a flower to put in your hair."

"Thank you," I say, standing much taller.

"My, my . . . " Nana says with a sigh.

I move as she tells each part of the dance that Emmadelle wrote down and sent in a letter. I stamp my feet slowly, raise arms and flip hands, just like the people I've seen in the picture, and snap . . . snap . . . snap my fingers.

My heels hit the hardwood. I clap like my heartbeat and dance . . . dance . . . dance like the ladies in Spain who do the flamenco. My great-aunty saw the dancers herself—the dancers who gave her the shawl from the shelf.

I follow them, digging my toes before stepping. I prance as I dance.
With my chin in the air, I look at the floor, and I hear Nana saying,
"More, señorita! More!"

The dancers beside me, we clap-ap together. We sway to the rhythm and watch the fringe fall. I twirl in a Spanish shawl worn at a bullfight and stamp . . . stamp . . . stamp to the story that Nana has told me again and again.

"Then Emmadelle wrapped up the shawl," I say. "And she mailed it to you along with a letter."

"That's right," Nana says. "You know it by heart."

"But I never read what was said in the letter," I say very slowly. "Do you still have it?"

"Why, yes," Nana says. "Would you like to see it? Now that you're eight and know to be careful, I'll let you read it, if that's what you want."

Nana and I go into the attic and open a trunk that weighs more than I do. Inside are bundles of ribbon-wrapped letters, tall stacks of sketchbooks, and piles of old papers. Nana finds the right letter in just a few moments. It's written in cursive, but I can still read it.

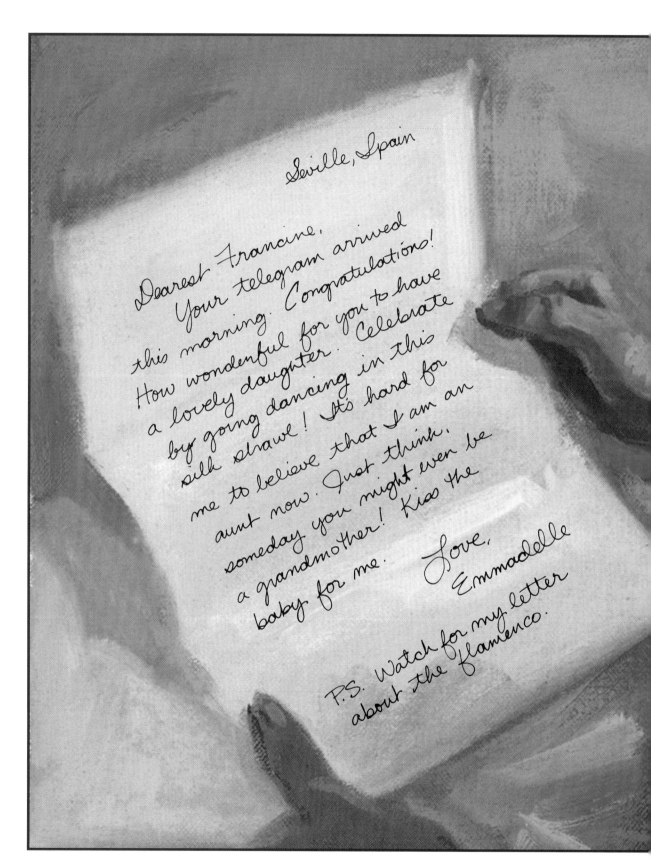

Seville, Spain

Dearest Francine,
    Your telegram arrived
this morning. Congratulations!
How wonderful for you to have
a lovely daughter. Celebrate
by going dancing in this
silk shawl! It's hard for
me to believe that I am an
aunt now. Just think,
someday you might even be
a grandmother! Kiss the
baby for me.   Love,
                    Emmadelle

P.S. Watch for my letter
about the flamenco.

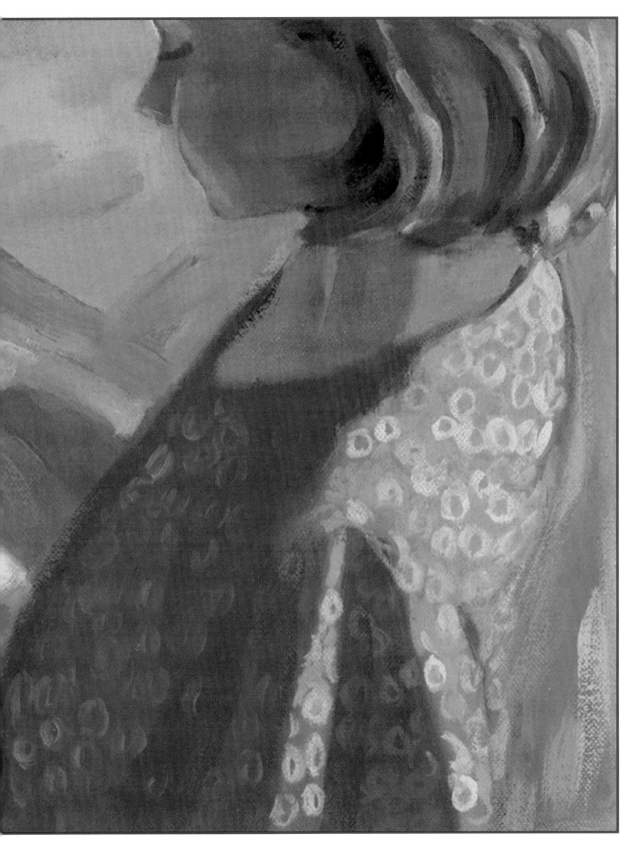

"The baby's my mother!" I giggle to think of her, wrapped up and gurgling in Nana's arms. "And I am the one who made you a grandmother. What did she say when I came along?"

"Had she been alive, she would have said, 'How delightful!'" Nana says laughing, tweaking my nose.

"I wish I had known her," I say.

"Oh, but you can," Nana says.

She turns to the trunk and opens a drawer filled with old pictures and black-and-white postcards. She starts a new story with, "My, my . . . how time does fly."

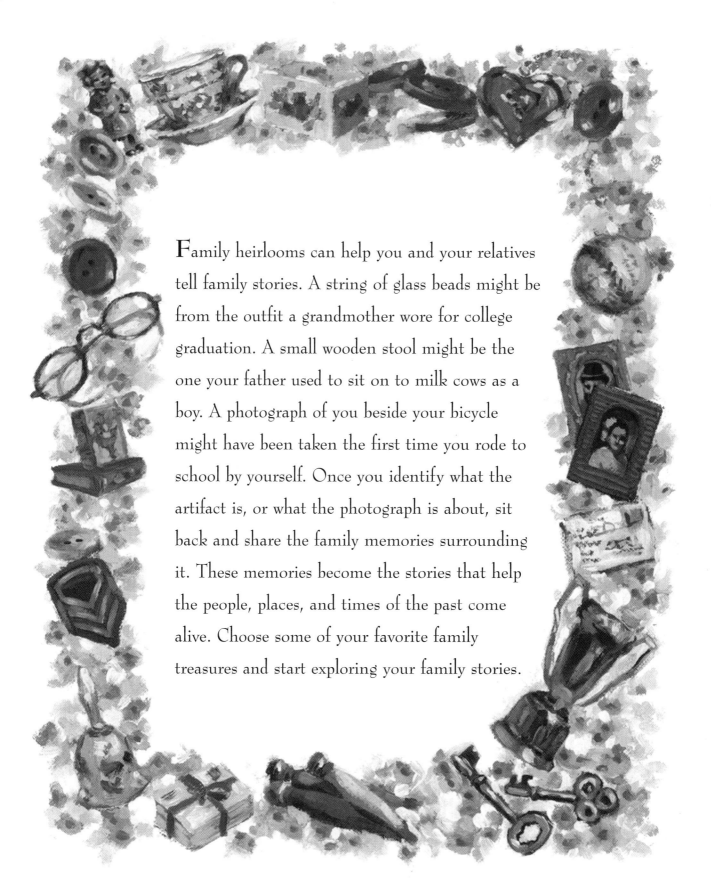

Family heirlooms can help you and your relatives tell family stories. A string of glass beads might be from the outfit a grandmother wore for college graduation. A small wooden stool might be the one your father used to sit on to milk cows as a boy. A photograph of you beside your bicycle might have been taken the first time you rode to school by yourself. Once you identify what the artifact is, or what the photograph is about, sit back and share the family memories surrounding it. These memories become the stories that help the people, places, and times of the past come alive. Choose some of your favorite family treasures and start exploring your family stories.